A Problem in Doodleland

WRITTEN AND ILLUSTRATED BY
KATHLEEN MURACA

Order this book online at www.trafford.com
or email orders@trafford.com

Most Trafford titles are also available at major online book retailers.

Trafford
PUBLISHING® www.trafford.com

North America & international
toll-free: 1 888 232 4444 (USA & Canada)
fax: 812 355 4082

Our mission is to efficiently provide the world's finest, most comprehensive book publishing service, enabling every author to experience success. To find out how to publish your book, your way, and have it available worldwide, visit us online at www.trafford.com

Because of the dynamic nature of the Internet, any web addresses or links contained in this book may have changed since publication and may no longer be valid. The views expressed in this work are solely those of the author and do not necessarily reflect the views of the publisher, and the publisher hereby disclaims any responsibility for them.

Any people depicted in stock imagery provided by Getty Images are models, and such images are being used for illustrative purposes only.
Certain stock imagery © Getty Images.

ISBN: 978-1-4907-9895-0 (sc)
ISBN: 978-1-4907-9894-3 (e)
ISBN: 978-1-4907-9985-8 (hc)

Library of Congress Control Number: 2019920981

Printed in the United States of America.

Trafford rev. 03/10/2020

A PROBLEM IN

DOODLELAND

Max,
This Book should put a smile
on your face. The Characters
have great personalities. Choose
a favorite.
Draw your favorite on the
Back colorful pages or just Doodle
and have fun.

Written and Illustrated by
Kathleen Muraca

One very hot day in Doodleland Melissa Mouse, Jenny Giraffe, Frankie Ferret, and Nickie the Nat sat around a large rock. They were trying to figure out what to do about a very serious problem.

"So, squeak, squeak, what do we do about this water problem we're having?" Asked Melissa Mouse.

"Water? Did anyone say Water?" Eddie Elephant asked, with his trunk held high in the air, sniffing for the clean scent of fresh water. He stomped through the long, dry, grass and joined the others.

"Yes, you heard the word water, but if your looking for some, we don't have any," answered Frankie Ferret.

"We need rain," Jenny Giraffe said, sticking her head high up into a cloud.

"Doodleland is doomed if we can't find a way to make it rain," Nickie the Nat said while flirting around Jenny's ear.

"Gee whizzles!" Squeaked Melissa Mouse, "Maybe we should go look for some."

"What did you think I was doing?" yelled Jenny Giraffe.

"You can't get any closer to rain then me." She stretched her neck as far up as it would go.

"Bumzer Doodle," cried Frankie Ferret. "Wait one minute,"

He interrupted. "Remember the old legend about Purple Doodle Mountain? My grandmother told me all about it,"

He continued. "She said, many, many years ago even before she was born; Doodleland was having trouble with its soil. Nothing would grow. The Doodle plants were all dying. There wasn't enough vegetation to go around. The Doodle animals were starving. According to legend, a group of Doodles went high up on Purple Doodle Mountain and that's where they found the answer."

"Well," squeaked Melissa Mouse, "What was the answer?"

"My grandmother said the group was gone for days and bright and early one morning they could see the Doodles coming down with wheel barrels filled with rich black soil. They mixed it with their own soil. Everything started growing again. Legend says it was magic soil and that a great Magician lives up there and he helped the Doodles with their problem." Frankie Ferret concluded.

"That's an old legend," piped Jenny Giraffe. "How do you know there is a great Magician on Purple Doodle Mountain?"

"Who cares," said Eddie Elephant. "Do you have a better idea?" Eddie asked Jenny.

"We still have some water left in the Doodle pond by old Harry Hippo's house," Jenny answered.

"I say let's go up to Purple Doodle Mountain before there isn't any left at all," Frankie Ferret replied.

"I agree," squeaked Melissa Mouse.

"Me too," fluttered Nickie the Nat.

"If that's what everyone wants," said Jenny Giraffe. "I guess you can count me in too."

They all started the long hike up to Purple Doodle Mountain. Grazing in the grass was Sharon Sheep and just above her head hanging on a branch was Sissy Snake taking a nap in the shade.

"What's all the ruckus about?" Sissy asked as she let out a deep yawn.

"Beats me," Sharon Sheep answered, " But it looks like all our friends are coming up Doodle road. There's Jenny Giraffe, Eddie Elephant, Nickie the Nat, and Frankie Ferret."

"Well, if Frankie Ferret is there, Melissa Mouse can't be far behind. She follows him everywhere." Sissy Snake said.

"It can't bother him much. I've never heard him object to all the attention she pays him." Sharon Sheep added.

When the group reached Sissy and Sharon, they explained about their journey and why.

Sissy Snake thought it was a good idea, but no one knew what they would find up on Purple Doodle Mountain. They just knew they couldn't sit around waiting for water to come to them. They had a mission and nothing was going to stop them.

As they traveled up the long hill toward the mountain, they sang songs and played word games.

Max the monkey was swinging from a tree and they all waved to him. He was playing with Gary Gorilla, who was close behind him.

It was beginning to get dark when suddenly from behind a bush out jumped Frank D. Fox and his faithful friend Stephanie Snail perched upon his back.

"Where is everyone sneaking off to without us?" Frank D. Asked loudly.

"Why don't you just give someone a heart attack while you're at it, jumping out of a bush like that?" Yelled Nicki the Nat.

"Talk about sneaking," squeaked Melissa Mouse.

"Okays, Okay, everyone put your skin back on. We didn't mean to scare you." Stephanie Snail interrupted.

"We just want to help. We heard about all of you going to Purple Doodle Mountain to possibly get water and we want to join you." Frank D. Fox added.

"Great," said Frankie Ferret.

"The more the merrier," chimed in Jenny Giraffe.

"It's getting darker by the minute, we better keep moving." Eddie Elephant remarked.

It was almost dark when they finally reached the top of Purple Doodle Mountain.

"I don't see anything up here." Jenny Giraffe was the first to speak up.

Everyone else was quiet. There wasn't anyone there but it was all so pretty. There were purple doodle flowers everywhere. The large Doodle trees had beautiful purple and yellow buds in full bloom.

"It's going to be very dark soon. We can't look for anyone until morning." Frankie Ferret said.

"That's fine with me," Sissy Snake replied as she slithered around the base of a tree. "I'm ready for sleep," she said.

Everyone nodded sleepily. It had been a long trip up to the mountain. Soon they were all fast asleep.

Melissa Mouse was the first one to wake up. One by one she woke the others. Purple Doodle Mountain was even more beautiful in the sunlight.

"Let's all look around. There are caves by that big peak on the mountain," said Frankie Ferret.

"Let's go explore," Nickie the Nat said flitting about.

"This place is cool, isn't it Stephanie?" Asked Frank D. Fox.

"It sure is," answered Stephanie snail.

They looked and looked for hours. They didn't find any Magician.

"I hate to say, I told you so, but, I told you so!" Jenny Giraffe ended.

"Oh, be quiet," yelled Nickie the Nat.

"No," yelled Jenny.

"Shut up," piped Frankie Ferret.

"Yeah," said Melissa Mouse.

Then Sissy snake and Sharon sheep began yelling. Frank D. Fox and Stephanie Snail joined in until it was the loudest shouting match you'd ever heard. They were all screaming at once and not one word could be understood.

Eddie Elephant stood just beneath the highest peak in the mountain. He started stamping his feet.

"Stop fighting," he yelled. They didn't hear him. He stamped his feet harder and harder until the mountain started to rumble.

Everyone stopped shouting and they all looked up at the peak watching Eddie Elephant stamp his feet.

The mountain rumbled again. Then rocks began to fall.

The mountain cracked open and water started pouring out of it like a water fall. Eddie Elephant looked like he was taking a shower.

Everyone watched in amazement. The water swooshed down the mountain.

"Let's go," yelled Jenny Giraffe.

They followed along side of the water as quickly as they could. Frank D. Fox was the fastest, with Stephanie Snail upon his back; he was running side by side with the water.

The water was filling the Doodle ponds and lakes. They could hear the other Doodle animals cheering in the distance.

"Water, "Ziggy Zebra was calling out to Harry Hippo.

"Water is coming down the mountain!" Leah Llama screamed to Betty Beaver.

"They did it," Billy Bear said to Bobby Beaver.

"I knew they would," Kathy Kangaroo remarked to Florence Flamingo.

"When they say they are going to do something, they really do it in a big way!" Tracy Turtle said to her friends Jaime and Joey Blue Jay.

"We sure do." The group called as they reached the bottom of the hill.

"But how? Was it magic?" Christopher Camel asked.

Eddie Elephant, Frankie Ferret, Melissa Mouse and the entire group all looked at each other and smiled.

"Well," Jenny Giraffe said, "I guess you could say it was the Magic of Loud voices and stomping feet."

The end